Michael Dahl

Tou Vue

Raint...

www.raintreepublishers.co.uk
Visit our website to find out
more information about
Raintree books.

To order:
Phone 0845 6044371
Fax +44 (0) 1865 312263
Email myorders@capstonepub.co.uk

Customers from outside the UK please telephone +44 1865 312262

Raintree is an imprint of Capstone Global Library
Limited, a company incorporated in England and Wales
having its registered office at 7 Pilgrim Street, London,
EC4V 6LB – Registered company number: 6695582

"Raintree" is a registered trademark
of Pearson Education Limited, under licence
to Capstone Global Library Limited

Text © Stone Arch Books 2009
First published in the United Kingdom in hardback
and paperback by Capstone Global Library in 2010
The moral rights of the proprietor have been asserted.

Creative Director: Heather Kindseth
Graphic Designer: Brann Garvey
UK Editor: Vaarunika Dharmapala
Originated by Capstone Global Library Ltd
Printed and bound in China by South China
Printing Company Ltd

ISBN 978 1 406215 12 0 (hardback)
14 13 12 11 10
10 9 8 7 6 5 4 3 2 1

ISBN 978 1 406215 26 7 (paperback)
14 13 12 11 10
10 9 8 7 6 5 4 3 2 1

British Library Cataloguing in Publication Data
A full catalogue record for this book is available from
the British Library.

CONTENTS

Introduction

A new Age of Dragons is about to begin. The powerful creatures will return to rule the world once more, but this time it will be different. This time, they will have allies who will help them. Around the world, some young humans are making a strange discovery. They are learning that they were born with dragon blood – blood that gives them amazing powers.

CHAPTER 1
Left Behind

A boy stood next to a car in a driveway.

"Your father will be sorry you couldn't come," said the boy's mother. Her hands were on the steering wheel.

"You look `terrible`, Henry," said the younger boy in the front seat.

"I feel `terrible`," said Henry, rubbing his arm.

"Go back to bed," said his mother. "It's just the flu. You can call your father tomorrow and wish him a **happy birthday**."

Will, the younger boy, handed
his brother a **comic book.**

"You can have this," Will said. It
was a new comic. Will hadn't even
read it yet.

"Thanks," said Henry. "I'll give it
back when I'm finished with it."

He *walked* weakly towards the
house. The car backed down the
driveway and drove off.

CHAPTER 2
Snow

The sky grew darker, and snow began to fall.

Soon, snow blanketed the road.

More snow blew on to the windscreen of the car.

"I think I should pull over," said Will's mum.

The car pulled into a small petrol station.

A **dark figure** sat inside the station, staring at them.

"Wait here, Will," said his mother.

As she walked into the station, Will watched the swirling snow.

CHAPTER 3
The White Thing

The light from the petrol station formed a small, *warm circle*.

Outside the circle, the snow became thicker and wilder.

Will wiped off the window.

He kept watching the snow.

Why was his mother taking so long?

Will heard a sound. It reminded
him of **thunder**.

Then he saw a shape moving
through the falling snow.

A white shape with **wings** passed over the petrol station.

Will jumped out of the car to get a better look.

"Will," cried his mother, running towards him. "Back in the car. We're going."

His mother drove out of the petrol station.

"That man was not very helpful," she told Will.

"He said that we have already passed the street your father lives on," Will's mother said.

"I'm sure he's wrong," she added.

Will's father had moved to another town.

This was the first time Will and his mother were visiting the new house.

CHAPTER 4
The Ditch

"There's something out there," said Will, quietly.

"What are you talking about?" asked his mother.

The snow was so heavy that they could not see the road ahead of them.

"Oh, great," said his mother. "The heater's broken!"

Will felt the car begin to **swerve**.

"Hold on!" shouted his mother.

CRUNCH!

The car slid into a snowy ditch.

"Will! You're bleeding," said his mother. He had hit his head against the window.

His mother couldn't find her mobile phone. It had fallen out of her purse when the car **crashed** into the ditch.

Will's head began to throb with pain.

We'll be stuck here forever, he thought.

If only Henry were here, he could help us.

CHAPTER 5
Getting A Lift

The car rocked.

"What's going on?" said his mother.

Will looked out. He saw a claw gripping one of the car windows.

His mother screamed.

Will thought he heard his name.

Then something whispered,

"Will, it's me!"

The car was lifted into the air.

The car swayed back and forth
in the snowy wind.

Will's mother clung tightly to
him.

Then, with a bump, the car was
back on the ground.

A *light* shone in front of them.

A man walked out of a lit up
house. He walked towards their car.

It was Will's father.

"We're here!" shouted Will.

"Did Henry come with you?"
asked Will's father.

His mother was too shocked to
speak.

Will followed his parents towards
the house.

A dark shape in the snow
caught his eye.

It was his **comic book.**

Somewhere in the storm above them, a fierce, happy roar shook the sky.

Of Dragons and Near-Dragons

If dragons truly lived on Earth, they would belong to the reptile family. Can reptiles survive through cold winters?

Reptiles cannot produce their own body heat. They must rely on outside sources like the Sun and warm air. In the winter, many reptiles hibernate. They stay in a sleepy state for many months, until the spring returns.

Sea turtles migrate to escape the cold weather. They swim to warmer waters in the southern hemisphere.

Lizards dig deep below the surface of the ground. They sleep in burrows or holes while the ground above them is frozen.

Some sand lizards hibernate below the ground until March or April. When they first come out of their holes, they look tired and pale. In a few weeks, after being in the sun, the lizards' skin turns a bright, healthy green.

ABOUT THE AUTHOR

Michael Dahl is the author of more than 200 books for children and young adults. He has won the AEP Distinguished Achievement Award three times for his non-fiction. His *Finnegan Zwake* mystery series was shortlisted twice by the Anthony and Agatha awards. He has also written the *Library of Doom* series. He is a featured speaker at conferences around the country on graphic novels and high-interest books for boys.

GLOSSARY

allies people or countries that give support to each other

clung held on to something tightly

creature living thing that is human or animal

fierce violent, strong, or dangerous

gripping holding on to something very tightly

rule have power over something

swerve change direction quickly

swirling moving in circles

throb beat loudly or rapidly

DISCUSSION QUESTIONS

1. If you were Will, would you have been afraid of the dragon?

2. Who was the dragon? What clues help you work this out?

3. Have you ever been caught in a storm? What was it like? How did you feel?

WRITING PROMPTS

1. Imagine Will tries to work out more about the dragon. Write a short story about his adventure.

2. Dragons are mythical creatures. Write a story about another mythical creature.

3. The title of a book can attract readers, as well as provide a description of the story. Think of three new titles for this book, choose your favourite, and explain why it's your pick.

MORE BOOKS TO READ

LIBRARY OF DOOM

Meet the mysterious Librarian. Keeper of the world's most dangerous books, sworn enemy of monsters made of paper and ink, crusader of young people threatened by ancient curses... Enter the Library of Doom to follow these heart-pounding adventures.

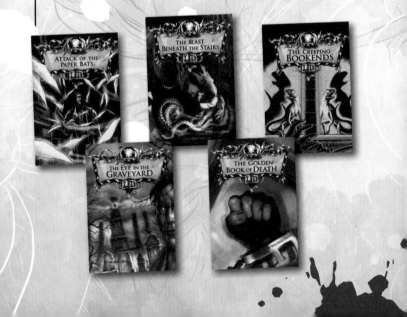